When Chocolate Milk Moved In

By Ken Harvey

Illustrations by MarySue Hermes

Design by schererMedia
Printed in China

Harvey, Ken.
    When chocolate milk moved in / Ken Harvey ;
illustrated by MarySue Hermes. — 1st ed.
        p. cm. — (Life in the 'fridge)
        SUMMARY: The foods inside a refrigerator learn about prejudice, respect and friendship when a new commodity—chocolate milk—moves in.
        Audience: Ages 4-6.
        Audience: Grades Pre-K to 1st.
        LCCN 2002104305
        ISBN 1-930093-16-0

    1. Prejudices—Juvenile fiction. 2. Respect—Juvenile fiction. 3. Friendship—Juvenile fiction.
4. Food—Juvenile fiction. [1. Prejudices—Fiction.
2. Respect—Fiction. 3. Friendship—Fiction. 4. Food—Fiction.]   I. Hermes, MarySue. II. Title.

PZ7.H267575Wh 2002   [E]
                QB102-701491

To my wife Janice and my boys
Anthony, Marcus & Nathaniel
—KH

To my parents, Tom and Mary Mertes,
who taught me to love.
—MSH

Once in a magical land there was a magical house. Inside that house, in a corner of the kitchen, stood a magical refrigerator, and inside that refrigerator all the food came to life!

Inside the 'fridge lived a friendly couple named Frank and Sally Gallon. They were gallons of milk.

Their best friend was Gus, a superstar sports drink.

A pint-sized juice drink named Billy the Kid lived there too. He was the youngest resident in the refrigerator.

The six Eggheads lived together in a carton. They were all very smart and loved to do math problems.

$$6 + 7 + 5 = 18$$

$$\begin{array}{r} 89 \\ -7 \\ \hline 82 \end{array}$$

$$\begin{array}{r} 12 \\ -5 \\ \hline 7 \end{array}$$

GRADE AA

$$3 \times 5 = 15$$

Armando, the refrigerator freshener, was the policeman.

He protected everyone from the Odor Boys who were always causing trouble.

On the top floor up in the freezer lived the Cool Cubes. These brothers were ice cubes who always wore sunglasses.

And finally, there were the Pops, the icicle
pops who had been around for a long time.
They were very wise, and you could always count
on them to help whenever there was a problem.

One day Frank and Sally Gallon were sitting quietly, enjoying the day while they watched Billy the Kid do flips and run around the 'fridge. They both wished they had his energy!

Sally looked at Frank and smiled, showing her pretty, white teeth. (As you know, milk gives you strong bones and healthy, white teeth.)

Frank gave his wife a hug. He loved her very much.

"What shall we do today?" Sally asked Frank. Frank thought about going to visit the Pops. He always enjoyed listening to their stories about the good old days.

But just as he was about to speak, the Odor Boys came walking over.

"Hey, Frank," one of them said. "Have you heard? We're getting a new neighbor!"

Frank looked surprised. He had been around for a while and usually knew about such big news before it happened. He also knew that if the Odor Boys were telling him about it, it probably meant trouble.

The Odor Boys ran away laughing, knowing they had planted the seeds of mischief.

The refrigerator door opened and the newcomer arrived. It was Chocolate Milk.

"Hello," he said to everyone. "My name is Fuller Chocolate."

Gus, the sports drink, was the first to greet him. "Hi," said Gus. "How's it going?"

"I'm doing fine," Mr. Chocolate replied.

When everyone else saw that Mr. Chocolate was friendly, they all hurried over to introduce themselves. Everyone, that is, except Frank Gallon. Sally Gallon introduced herself, but as she turned to introduce her husband, she realized he was not there. He was sitting in the corner.

"That's strange," Sally thought. "Maybe something is wrong with Frank."

Fuller Chocolate noticed Frank standing by himself and decided that Mr. Gallon must not like him. Maybe he thought he was too good to come over and introduce himself.

But that's really not what Frank was thinking. Truthfully, he was just a little bit shocked by what he saw. Mr. Chocolate looked different. He was darker. Frank had been around milk his entire life and had never seen dark milk. He didn't know what to think.

Sally Gallon waved to Frank, inviting him to come and meet Mr. Chocolate. Just as Frank started to walk toward them, the Odor Boys appeared again.

"Hey, Frank," one of them whispered. "Here is something to think about. Even though Mr. Chocolate is milk, he is different. He is a lot darker, and if milk is darker, how can it be good for you? Maybe he is sick or maybe something is wrong with him."

All the Odor Boys nodded in agreement. Then another one said, "I'd stay away from him if I were you—unless you want to end up looking like him!"

Even though Frank hadn't met Mr. Chocolate yet, he was scared. What if the Odor Boys were right?

Fuller Chocolate decided to take a walk around the 'fridge to look at the rest of the shelves. While he was gone, everyone rushed over to Frank to ask him what was wrong. Frank told them what the Odor Boys had said.

They all sat down in shock. They hadn't thought about Mr. Chocolate being different.

Then Gus stood up. "Wait a minute!" he said. "In sports, everyone drinks sports drinks like me. We are all different too—different sizes, different flavors—even different colors. Being different doesn't mean there is something wrong with us."

Gus had made a good point, but then Frank stood up and said, "That's easy for you to say. None of you is milk. I *am* milk and I could end up like Mr. Chocolate!"

Billy the Kid spoke next and said something pretty smart for someone who was only pint-sized. "Mr. Gallon, even if you *did* end up like Mr. Chocolate, what would be wrong with that?"

Everyone was quiet.

Fuller Chocolate was heading back to the group when the Odor Boys stopped him to introduce themselves. "Hello," they said, trying to sound nice. "We are the Odor Boys."

Then one of them whispered, "We all like you, but what's wrong with that Frank fellow? We heard him say that he was better than you," he lied. "He thinks he's too good to talk to you."

"What?!" Mr. Chocolate shouted. He was very angry. "I don't even know him and he already thinks he's better than me? Wait until I see him. I'll give him a piece of my mind!"

Fuller stomped off to find Frank.

The Odor Boys looked at one another and laughed. They knew they had started all this trouble and now there might even be a fight!

Meanwhile, Frank thought about what Billy the Kid and the others had told him, and he decided they were right. He was just being silly.

He wished that he had never listened to the Odor Boys.

Frank saw Mr. Chocolate walking toward him.
"Good," he thought. "Now I can apologize for the
way I acted."

But before he could say a word, Mr. Chocolate
started yelling at him.

Everyone was surprised, especially when Frank
began yelling back at Mr. Chocolate. They all worried
that there might be a fistfight.

The Odor Boys arrived. They were laughing and
looking pleased with themselves because they knew
they had caused all the trouble.

Just then Armando and the Pops arrived on the scene. Armando chased the Odor Boys away. The Pops began talking to Frank and Mr. Chocolate trying to calm them down.

"We have been around for a long, long time,"
Red Pop said, "so listen to us."

"Why are you two fighting?" asked Green Pop. "We are all different colored icicle pops, yet we are all brothers. We may taste different, but we serve the same purpose. We make people smile! Use your minds and judge each other not on how you look, but on what is inside your hearts."

Once again, the Pops had shared their wisdom.

Frank and Fuller Chocolate looked at each other and smiled. They knew they had been foolish to listen to the Odor Boys. They shook hands and have been best friends ever since that day.

How good and pleasant it is when brothers live together in unity.

Psalms 133:1